The Lady and the Spider

W9-BKN-965

ALSO BY FAITH McNULTY

How to Dig a Hole to the Other Side of the World
pictures by Marc Simont

Hurricane
pictures by Gail Owens

Mouse and Tim
pictures by Marc Simont

Peeping in the Shell: A Whooping Crane Is Hatched
pictures by Irene Brady

Whales: Their Life in the Sea
pictures by John Schoenherr

I CAN READ BOOKS®

The Elephant Who Couldn't Forget
pictures by Marc Simont

Woodchuck
pictures by Joan Sandin

The Lady and the Spider

by Faith McNulty

illustrated by Bob Marstall

A Harper Trophy Book
Harper & Row, Publishers

Library of Congress Cataloging in Publication Data
McNulty, Faith
   The lady and the spider.

   Summary: A spider who lives in a head of
lettuce is saved when the lady who finds her puts
her back into the garden.
   1. Children's stories, American.   2. Spiders—
Juvenile fiction.   [1. Spiders—Fiction]
I. Marstall, Bob, ill.   II. Title.
PZ10.3.M456Lad   1986   [E]   85-5427
ISBN 0-06-024191-8
ISBN 0-06-024192-6 (lib. bdg.)

(A Harper Trophy book)
ISBN 0-06-443152-5 (pbk.)

Designed by Al Cetta
First Harper Trophy Edition, 1987

To Richard Martin,
with all my love

On a summer day
in a lady's garden,
a spider stood on
a lettuce leaf.

She looked about and saw
hills of green
and valleys of green.
Between two leaves
she saw a green cave.
Walking daintily
on her eight legs,
she went inside.

With the tips
of her long front legs,
she felt the sides and
the ceiling and the floor.
The cave suited her.
It was a leafy den
just the right size
to be her home.

When night came, dew formed on the leaves.
Drops of water trickled into a hollow
beside the spider's den.
They made a tiny pool.

The moon rose.
Moths wakened and flew
dizzily about the garden
in search of other moths.
One saw moonlight shine
in the pool. It flew into the water.
Its wings became wet.
Unable to fly, it drowned.

In the morning
when the sun rose,
the spider looked into the pool
and saw the moth.
She walked to the water's edge
and had breakfast.

Each day the lady came
to tend her garden.
She planted seeds,
and pulled up weeds,
and sprinkled water.
She looked among the leaves
for bugs. She did not want
bugs to eat her garden.
Once she saw the spider walking
on a leaf but paid no heed. She
knew spiders do not eat lettuce.

When the lady's footsteps
shook the ground,
the spider ran and hid.
One day the lady's dress
brushed the leaves around
the spider's home. The spider felt
an earthquake, but the lady
did not know what she had done.

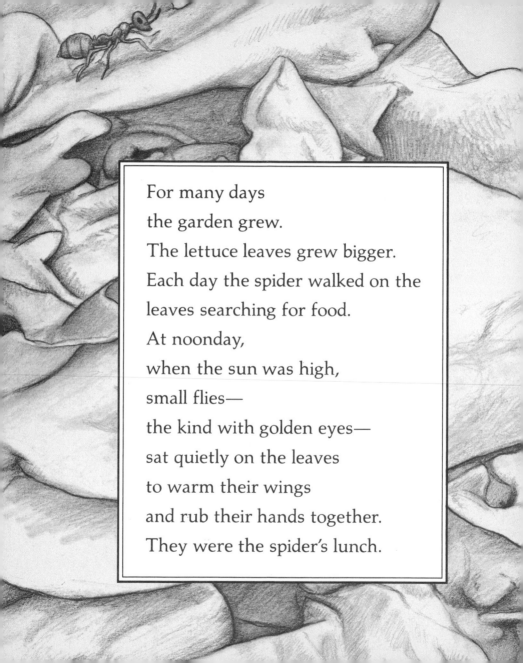

For many days
the garden grew.
The lettuce leaves grew bigger.
Each day the spider walked on the
leaves searching for food.
At noonday,
when the sun was high,
small flies—
the kind with golden eyes—
sat quietly on the leaves
to warm their wings
and rub their hands together.
They were the spider's lunch.

Birds also dined in the lady's garden.
They perched on the fence and looked
about sharply,
peering here and there,
searching for bugs.

One day the spider was having lunch.

She was eating a large blue fly.

A bird swooped down.

Just in time, the spider saw

its swift, dark shadow.

She leaped into her den.

The bird flew off with the fly.

As the days grew hot,
the lady knew it was time
to pick the lettuce.
Each day she came to the garden
with a basket and a knife
and cut off a head of lettuce
for her lunch.

Each day the lettuce
that she picked
was closer to the head of lettuce
in which the spider lived.

One day, when the sun came up
and warmed the walls
of her den,
the spider went out and walked down a green hill
to her sparkling pond
to see what might be there
for breakfast.
Just at that moment
the lady came into the garden.
She bent down,
grasped the head of lettuce
in which the spider lived, and cut it
off at the roots.
She shook off the dew drops.
She put the lettuce
with the spider hidden among its leaves
into her basket.
Of course the lady had no idea
the spider was there.

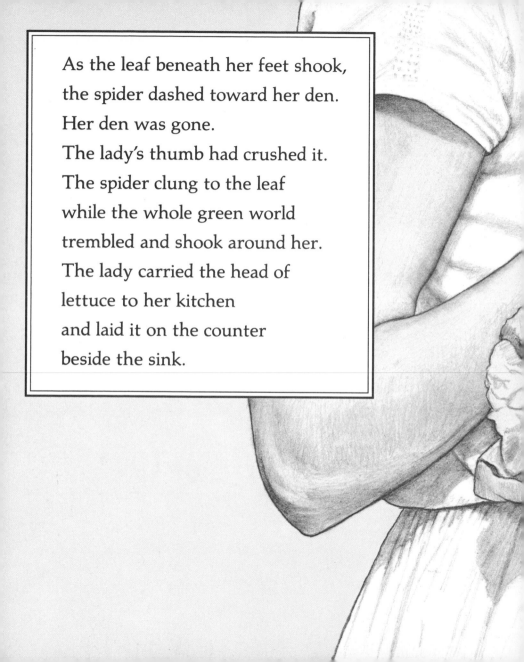

As the leaf beneath her feet shook,
the spider dashed toward her den.
Her den was gone.
The lady's thumb had crushed it.
The spider clung to the leaf
while the whole green world
trembled and shook around her.
The lady carried the head of
lettuce to her kitchen
and laid it on the counter
beside the sink.

When her world became still,
the spider stood up
and walked about
among the leaves.
She tried to see with her eight eyes.
She tried to feel with the tips of
her legs. She tried to think
with her tiny brain.
It was no use.

The spider could not know
that she had made her home
in a head of lettuce
in a lady's garden,
and that the lady intended
to eat that lettuce for lunch.

The lady bent over the sink.
She picked up the lettuce.
She parted the leaves and looked for bugs.
She did not see the spider,
crouched deep in a dark cranny
between two leaves.

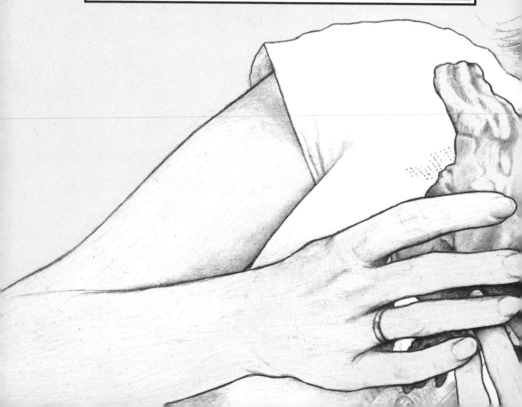

The lady put the lettuce into the sink.
She put in the stopper
and turned on the water.
It poured clean and cold over the leaves.

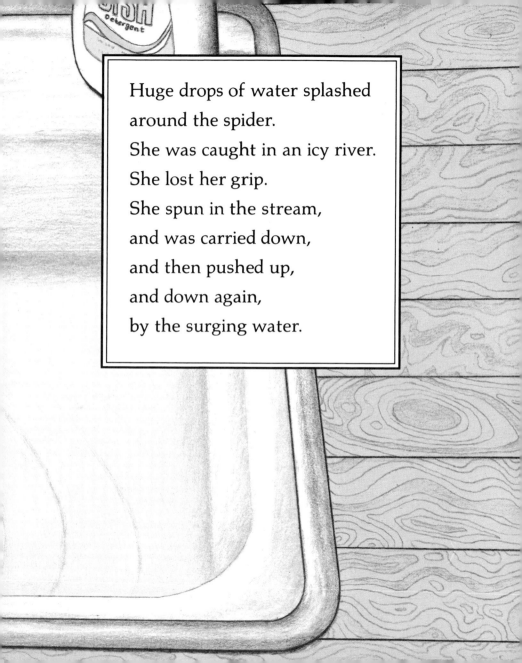

Huge drops of water splashed
around the spider.
She was caught in an icy river.
She lost her grip.
She spun in the stream,
and was carried down,
and then pushed up,
and down again,
by the surging water.

The lady turned off the faucet.
The water in the sink became calm.
The head of lettuce floated,
rocking on tiny waves.
Part of it was under water
and part above.
The spider struggled upward
to the surface.
Her front legs found the edge
of a leaf.
She was heavy with water.
With all her strength
she pulled herself up
onto a leafy island.

The leaf was cold.
It was wet.
The spider walked about,
waving her long front legs,
searching for a dark, dry, safe
place to hide.

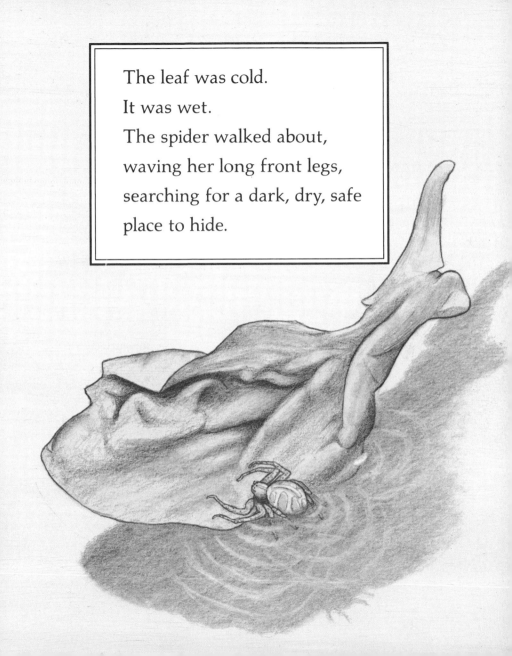

The lady looked down,
and a tiny motion caught her eye.
She saw a small spider,
adrift on a raft of lettuce,
trying to escape.
The lady picked up the leaf
with the spider clinging to it
and opened the lid
of the garbage pail.

Just before the leaf
dropped from her fingers,
a thought crossed her mind.
She looked again at the spider.
The spider, searching for
a place to hide,
waved her legs.
She waved and waved and waved.

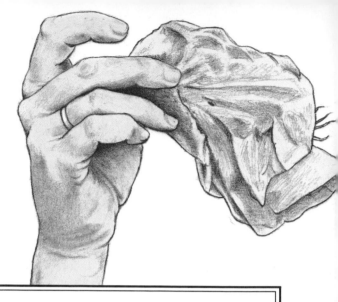

Looking closely, the lady saw
things she had never noticed before.
She saw how the spider's color matched
the leaves. She saw the tiny dots
that were her eyes.
She saw how delicately she moved
on her slender legs
and how she
waved and waved and waved.

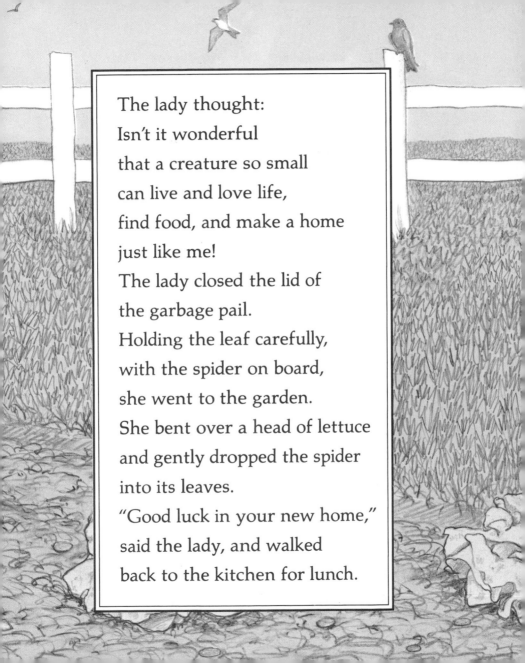

The lady thought:
Isn't it wonderful
that a creature so small
can live and love life,
find food, and make a home
just like me!
The lady closed the lid of
the garbage pail.
Holding the leaf carefully,
with the spider on board,
she went to the garden.
She bent over a head of lettuce
and gently dropped the spider
into its leaves.
"Good luck in your new home,"
said the lady, and walked
back to the kitchen for lunch.

The spider landed lightly
in a sun-warmed,
sweet-smelling valley.
She sat still until she
was warm and dry.
Then she walked up a green hill
and down a green hill,
searching with the tips
of her long front legs.